Jeremy Ja

Backya

Pirates Don't Change Diapers

Pirates Don't Change Diapers

WRITTEN BY

Melinda Long

ILLUSTRATED BY

David Shannon

Harcourt, Inc.

Orlando Austin New York San Diego Toronto London

Printed in Singapore

irates don't change diapers. They don't even change socks!
I know because I used to be a pirate, but that's another story.

Today, while I was wondering what to buy my mother for her birthday with the twenty-seven cents in my pocket, Mom came into the room. "Jeremy Jacob," she said, "I have to go get some milk. Your dad's taking a nap, so try not to bother him." As she went out the door, she called, "If your sister wakes up, try to keep her happy. I'll be back soon."

Oh, great, I thought. *Keeping that baby happy is never easy.*

Mom had hardly been gone a minute when I heard a knock on the door. I peeked through the peephole.

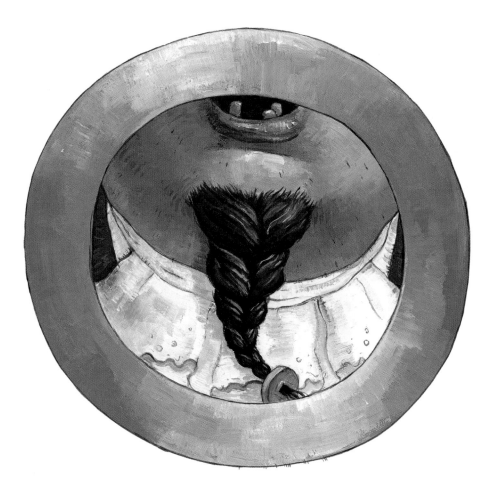

There were some old friends on the front porch!

"Ahoy thar, Jeremy Jacob. Are we ever glad to see you!" said Captain Braid Beard. "We've run into a boatload of trouble. Our ship ran aground on a coral reef. The bow broke open and our figurehead's nose tore right off! I had it carved special to look just like me blessed mother, too."

"Aye, his mother!"

the crew chorused.

"It'll have to be replaced, and that'll cost us a pretty penny,"
Braid Beard said. "We be needin' the treasure we buried in your
backyard!"

"Treasure!" the pirates repeated.

What with all that yelling, my baby sister woke up. It's a miracle
my dad didn't wake up, too.

"Aargh!" hollered Braid Beard. "What be that caterwaulin'?"

"That's Bonney Anne," I said, "and I'm supposed to keep her quiet. You'll have to help me babysit."

"Babysit?" Braid Beard scratched his head. "Pirates don't sit on babies!"

"No sittin' on babies!"

hollered the crew.

But there was no way we'd be digging up the treasure, I told them, until Bonney Anne was happy again.

That's how the pirates became babysitters.

Bonney Anne always has her diaper changed after her nap—
but the pirates needed a lot of practice. Things got really interesting
when we ran out of diapers.

Then it was Bonney Anne's lunchtime. And when she gets hungry, everybody knows it.

Braid Beard sniffed the baby food. "Shiver me timbers!" he yelled. "What be this vile-smellin' swill?"

"Strained spinach," I told him.

"Strained spinach!" Braid Beard said. "A bilge rat wouldn't eat this stuff!" Then Bonney Anne sneezed. I got out of the way just in time.

"Aargh! Strained spinach!"

wailed the pirates.

When Bonney Anne was finally changed and fed, we thought we'd be able to get outside to dig. But every time we tried to sneak away, the baby got fussy again. She does that a lot!

"Now what does the wee mutineer want?" Braid Beard demanded.

"Maybe you should rock her," I said.

"Aye then!" bellowed Braid Beard. "Rock on, me hearties!"

"Rock on!"

cheered the crew.

"Not that kind of rock!" I groaned. "Use the rocking chair!"

When rocking didn't work, we tried pirate peekaboo.

We danced a pirate jig.

We sang sea chanteys.

"Look!" I whispered. "She's falling asleep again! Quick, let's dig up the treasure now!"

"Time to dig, laddies!" commanded Braid Beard.

"Shush!" I said. "Not so loud!"

"Not so loud!" roared the pirates.

Bonney Anne caterwauled until we found the only person
who could keep her quiet. Quicker than you can say "scurvy dog,"
we headed out the door to get the treasure.

"The map!" said Braid Beard. "Hand over the map!"

"The map?"

Everybody emptied their pockets. No luck.

"The wee lass! She must have it!" Braid Beard hollered, and we
all ran for the house.

But the map wasn't there.

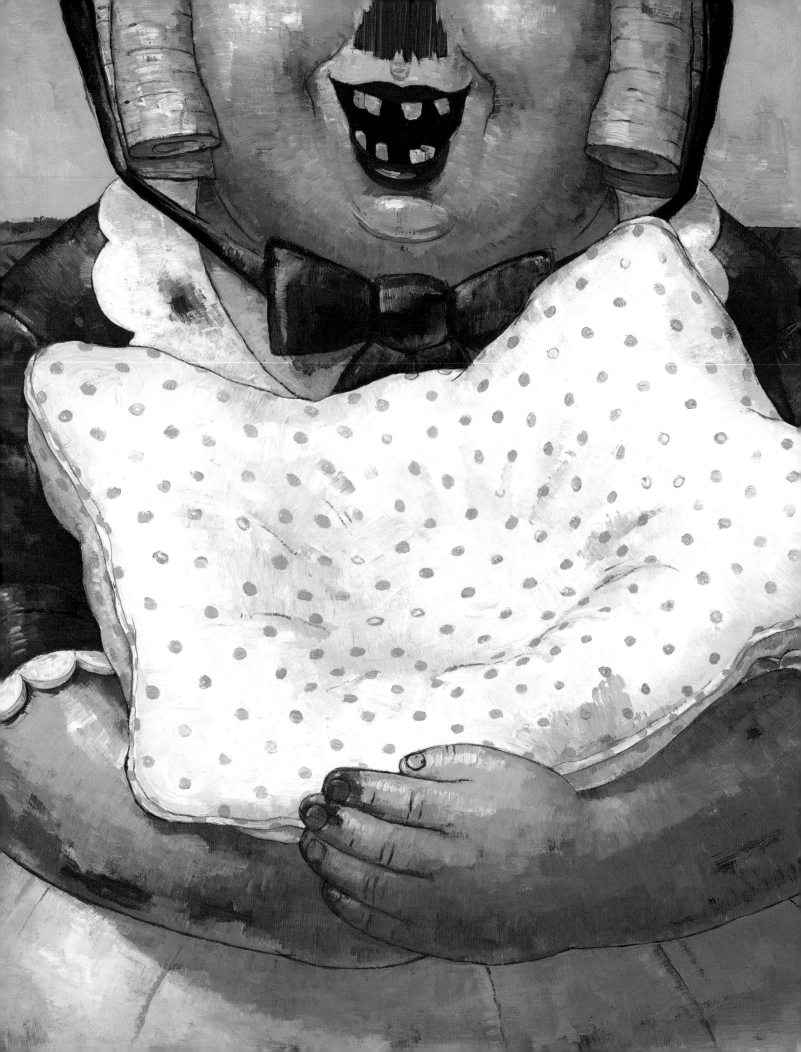

Neither was Bonney Anne.
"The map!" cried Braid Beard.

"The treasure!"

boomed the crew.

"THE BABY!"

I yelled louder than anyone. After all, she *is* my sister. And I was getting really worried.

We searched all over the house, then ran back outside.
We stopped so fast we were almost pirate pancakes. There was
Bonney Anne. And she had the map.

"Avast!" yelled Braid Beard. "The wee lass has eaten it!
Now we'll never be able to fix the ship! We're marooned!"

"Marooned!"

moaned the others.

"Maybe not," I said. "Thanks to my little sister, I think I know exactly where to dig!"

With all of us digging, we found the treasure in no time.
Braid Beard opened the chest and grinned. "Choose yer reward,
Jeremy Jacob! Ye've earned yer fair share." It didn't take me long
to decide. Green is my mom's favorite color.

"If you need a babysitter again, matey," Braid Beard said,
"you know how to find us! Just run the Jolly Roger up yonder
pole."

"*Up yonder pole!*" I shouted.

As the pirates headed back to their ship, Bonney Anne and I
ran straight for the house.

We had a birthday present to wrap.

For Papa Long, the coolest
pirate of them all—we miss you
—M. L.

For Baby Quinlan, who comes
from good pirate stock, has four teeth,
and loaned me a diaper to draw
—D. S.

Text copyright © 2007 by Melinda Long
Illustrations copyright © 2007 by David Shannon

www.HarcourtBooks.com

Library of Congress Cataloging-in-Publication Data
Long, Melinda.
Pirates don't change diapers/written by Melinda Long;
illustrated by David Shannon.
p. cm.
Summary: Braid Beard and his pirate crew return to retrieve the treasure they
buried in Jeremy Jacob's backyard, but first they must help calm his baby sister,
Bonney Anne, whom they awoke from her nap.
[1. Babysitters—Fiction. 2. Pirates—Fiction.
3. Babies—Fiction.] I. Shannon, David, 1959– ill. II. Title.
PZ7.L856Pir 2007
[E]—dc22   2005021119
ISBN 978-0-15-205353-6

HGFEDC

Printed in Singapore

The illustrations in this book were done in acrylic on illustration board.
The display lettering was created by Jane Dill.
The text type was set in Packard Bold.
Color separations by Bright Arts Ltd., Hong Kong
Printed and bound by Tien Wah Press, Singapore
This book was printed on totally chlorine-free Stora Enso Matte paper.
Production supervision by Jane Van Gelder
Designed by Scott Piehl

Many thanks to David, Jeannette, and Steve, my conspirators;
to Cathy and Bryan, for "pirate peekaboo"; to Mark and my mother,
for confusing the pirates even more; and to my dad, for the storytelling
gene. As always, my love and thanks go to my ever-patient husband,
Thom, for his constant support and encouragement. I'd set sail with
the lot of you any day! —M. L.